Samuel French Acting

Bull in a China Shop

by Bryna Turner

SAMUELFRENCH.COM   SAMUELFRENCH.CO.UK

FOR PRODUCTION ENQUIRIES

UNITED STATES AND CANADA
Info@SamuelFrench.com
1-866-598-8449

UNITED KINGDOM AND EUROPE
Plays@SamuelFrench.co.uk
020-7255-4302

Each title is subject to availability from Samuel French, depending upon country of performance. Please be aware that *BULL IN A CHINA SHOP* may not be licensed by Samuel French in your territory. Professional and amateur producers should contact the nearest Samuel French office or licensing partner to verify availability.

MUSIC USE NOTE

Licensees are solely responsible for obtaining formal written permission from copyright owners to use copyrighted music in the performance of this play and are strongly cautioned to do so. If no such permission is obtained by the licensee, then the licensee must use only original music that the licensee owns and controls. Licensees are solely responsible and liable for all music clearances and shall indemnify the copyright owners of the play(s) and their licensing agent, Samuel French, against any costs, expenses, losses and liabilities arising from the use of music by licensees. Please contact the appropriate music licensing authority in your territory for the rights to any incidental music.

IMPORTANT BILLING AND CREDIT REQUIREMENTS

If you have obtained performance rights to this title, please refer to your licensing agreement for important billing and credit requirements.

BULL IN A CHINA SHOP premiered on February 11, 2017 at Lincoln Center Theater at the Claire Tow in New York City. The performance was directed by Lee Sunday Evans, with sets by Arnulfo Maldonado, costumes by Oana Botez, lighting by Eric Southern, and sound by Broken Chord. The stage manager was Megan Schwarz Dickert. The cast was as follows:

WOOLLEY	Enid Graham
MARKS	Ruibo Qian
DEAN WELSH	Lizbeth Mackay
PEARL	Michele Selene Ang
FELICITY	Crystal Lucas-Perry

CHARACTERS

WOOLLEY (MARY) – The swagger of a gunslinger buttoned into an ankle-length dress; a confident and caring partner to Marks.

MARKS (JEANNETTE) – A moody and fitful writer and partner, an enigmatic teacher; Woolley's former student and current partner, ten years Woolley's junior.

DEAN WELSH – A tight-lipped New England type. Woolley's subordinate, but Marks' superior.

PEARL – The president of a secret society of fangirls of the relationship between Marks and Woolley, Marks' obsessively devoted student.

FELICITY – Marks' roommate in a house off campus called Sweet Pea. A professor in the Philosophy department.

SETTING

Various locations in and around an old Massachusetts seminary-turned-university.

TIME

Between 1899 and 1937.

AUTHOR'S NOTES

A note about pace

We move through forty years in ninety minutes, which requires a certain pace, a certain energy. An inkling of: "How did that happen?" "When did we make that turn?" The feeling of: "One second ago I could have sworn we were two entirely different people." Or maybe: "How dare you grow without me?" Or maybe: "Why are you changing I don't think I'm changing am I changing?"

A note about casting

This is an excavation of queer history, a history that has been buried and hidden and kept from us. It's also a queering of history, a look at past events through a contemporary gaze. Queering history entails making room for the people who have been routinely denied a place in the narrative. There are no white men in this play, but it should not be filled entirely with white women either. This play is filled with purposeful anachronisms. That's part of the point. This is a startlingly contemporary play.

A note about punctuation

The scenes that have less capitalization and punctuation are intended to communicate either greater intimacy and less formality between characters, or moments of poetry.

*Inspired by the real letters between Mary Woolley and
Jeannette Marks spanning from 1899 to 1937*

1.

(Darkness.)

(A single light up on **MARY WOOLLEY**.*)*

(She's a bull in a china shop.)

(She's got the swagger of a gunslinger buttoned into an ankle-length dress.)

(It's 1899.)

WOOLLEY. Listen.

I'm a bull in a china shop.

You give me a struggling women's seminary,

I'll give you the fucking preeminent school of critical social thought for women.

You want a training ground for good pious wives?

Fuck that.

I'll give you fully evolved human beings.

So you're afraid they won't find husbands?

So what.

I say: If a man is interested in headless women, send him to France.

> *(Lights up on the rest of the room.)*
>
> *(A tiny apartment.)*
>
> (**JEANNETTE MARKS** *is helping* **WOOLLEY** *practice for her interview.)*

MARKS. That's a little...

WOOLLEY. What?

MARKS. Strong.

WOOLLEY. I want strong.

MARKS. Maybe too strong?

WOOLLEY. You think?

MARKS. I mean.

It *is* a seminary.

WOOLLEY. Right.

MARKS. So the whole pious wives thing...

They kind of want that.

WOOLLEY. Yeah, but I'm saying we could

expand that concept.

MARKS. It kind of sounds like you're advocating for women
to tell men to go fuck themselves.

WOOLLEY. You think that's too strong?

MARKS. Who's on the hiring committee?

WOOLLEY. Good point.

MARKS. Why do you even want this job?

WOOLLEY. I'd be the president.

MARKS. Of a regional seminary.

WOOLLEY. The president.

MARKS. But you're such a great professor.

You're already on track to become a dean.

WOOLLEY. Wellesley doesn't need me.

Holyoke needs me.

MARKS. Because it's failing.

WOOLLEY. Which means: they're ready for change!

This is a chance to rebuild an institution from the
ground up.

To question the foundations,

to give women the tools to free themselves

from their subservient position in the world.

This is it.

Revolution.

MARKS. You want a revolution?

WOOLLEY. I am a revolution.

(**WOOLLEY** *pulls* **MARKS** *into bed.*)

MARKS. What am I going to do if you go to smelly Holyoke?

WOOLLEY. Come with me.

MARKS. What do you mean come with you?

WOOLLEY. I mean: come with me.

> I want you there.
> I need you there.
> Right by my side.

MARKS. So *you* get the revolution,
> and *I* get to be the headless wife.

WOOLLEY. I didn't say that.

MARKS. I'm supposed to give up my education?
> To follow you?
> To Holyoke?

WOOLLEY. You could finish your thesis there!

MARKS. What am I supposed to do in the middle of nowhere?

WOOLLEY. Teaching experience.
> For your résumé.

MARKS. I don't want to be a fucking teacher.

WOOLLEY. I know.
> It would just be to get by.
> While you write.
> The great American whatever.

MARKS. They do say *nature* is good for writers.

WOOLLEY. A writer's retreat.

MARKS. In the president's house.

WOOLLEY. Abso-fucking-lutely.

> *(They kiss.)*

MARKS. I don't know.
> It's complicated...

WOOLLEY. Look:
> I love you.
> I'll always love you.
> What's complicated about that?

2.

(Inside the office of the president.)

(PRESIDENT WOOLLEY *and* **DEAN WELSH.)**

WELSH. Well, it's complicated...

WOOLLEY. I love complicated.

WELSH. *Some* of the faculty are concerned that
you might show a sort of favoritism towards
Ms. Marks.

WOOLLEY. That's absurd.

WELSH. They are concerned about her recent appointment
to Chair of the English department.

WOOLLEY. I think Ms. Marks will be fresh blood in a stagnant
department.

WELSH. Yes.

Very fresh blood.

She's hardly been here a year.

WOOLLEY. Dean Welsh.

When I took this job, I said I'd be making some changes.

WELSH. You did.

WOOLLEY. I'm interested in Revolution.

WELSH. I remember you said that.

WOOLLEY. Fresh blood.

New ideas.

All of it.

We need it if we are to survive the turn of the century.

WELSH. And I understand that.

I appreciate your vision.

And yet, the *faculty*, they are concerned about Ms.
Marks.

WOOLLEY. How so?

WELSH. Well, for starters, they say she has no real interest
in the school.

WOOLLEY. That's absurd.

WELSH. She skips office hours.

She treats department meetings with disdain – at best.

WOOLLEY. Who doesn't treat department meetings with disdain?

WELSH. She wrote this note on her syllabus for Lit 101:

"All preconceived notions of genre must be questioned.

The canon is suspect.

The invisible line between teacher and student must be washed away.

Therefore, and therein, we will all begin the long tangled process of unlearning."

WOOLLEY. She's inspired.

WELSH. She's creating problems.

WOOLLEY. I'm interested in her leadership.

WELSH. The word "leadership" seems...strong.

We've noticed that she and her students spend class time smoking cigarettes outside the library.

WOOLLEY. She says it increases circulation in the brain.

WELSH. We have professors who have been here upwards of ten years.

Twenty even.

They are not taking this rejection lightly.

WOOLLEY. Revolution, Welsh.

If we want to change the world, first we have to question it.

Ms. Marks is an excellent example of what I'm trying to do here.

WELSH. There is...one other observation.

WOOLLEY. Yes?

WELSH. It hasn't exactly gone...*unobserved* that you climb three flights of stairs each night
to kiss Ms. Marks goodnight.

WOOLLEY. And?

WELSH. They've noticed, that's all.

3. *

*(**MARKS** is teaching a lit class. You're in it. So is **PEARL**.)*

MARKS. "He – for there could be no doubt of his sex, though the fashion of the time did something to disguise it – was in the act of slicing at the head of a Moor which swung from the rafters."

Why is this the first line of *Orlando*?

I'll read it again.

"He, m-dash, for there could be no doubt of his sex, though the fashion of the time did something to disguise it, m-dash, was in the act of slicing at the head of a Moor which swung from the rafters."

She only gets out a pronoun before she interrupts herself.
She says "He" and then feels so compelled to defend his sex that she interrupts herself, telling us not to doubt it.

Why?

Because she wants us to think about that which we usually don't think.
In assuring us, she's actually destabilizing us.

"He – for there could be no doubt of his sex."

It's as if I brought you to my house and the first thing I told you was:
"There are no skeletons in any of my closets."

Why would I dismiss a doubt that hadn't yet been raised?
Any sane person would immediately begin opening the closets.

---

*Excerpt from *Orlando* given by permission of The Society of Authors, the Literary Representative of the Estate of Virginia Woolf.

Just so, Woolf wants you to begin to question the unquestionable.

"He – for there could be no doubt of his sex."

doubt he
doubt sex
doubt gender
doubt language
doubt everything

"He – for there could be no doubt of his sex."

Welcome to Woolf, my children.

Yes, Pearl?

4.

(**WOOLLEY** *climbs three flights of stairs to kiss* **MARKS** *goodnight.*)

(*She knocks on* **MARKS**' *door.*)

(*They kiss.*)

MARKS. Stay.

WOOLLEY. I can't.

MARKS. I hate this stupid place.

WOOLLEY. It's not that bad.

MARKS. Maybe for you, Madam President.

WOOLLEY. I prefer just "President."

MARKS. I can't believe I have to live in faculty housing.

WOOLLEY. It's temporary.

MARKS. Everyone here is old.

WOOLLEY. I'm working on that...

But you! Your students worship you.

I read your evaluations today.

Someone wrote a sonnet about your eyes.

MARKS. What was the final couplet?

WOOLLEY. Something dreadful.

MARKS. It must have been Pearl.

WOOLLEY. I had a little talk with Dean Welsh again...

MARKS. The faculty hate me.

So what.

WOOLLEY. Do you really treat department meetings with disdain?

MARKS. It's like being forced to attend weekly funerals for higher education.

WOOLLEY. Maybe you could practice smiling more?

MARKS. Is there something I should be smiling about?

WOOLLEY. Well, the campus is very beautiful.

MARKS. Yes, the shadows in the cave are stunning.

WOOLLEY. This nihilism.

It's sort of out of place in a seminary.

MARKS. I'm out of place in a seminary.

WOOLLEY. We're changing it.

But maybe while we do, we could practice smiling more.

MARKS. Don't patronize me, *Madam* President.

WOOLLEY. I'm sorry.

I'm just trying to make things go more smoothly.

MARKS. Who ever heard of a smooth revolution?

WOOLLEY. You're right.

You're right.

MARKS. Stay.

WOOLLEY. I can't.

There will be talk.

MARKS. There is already talk.

WOOLLEY. When the president's house is ready, everything will be easier.

MARKS. The rumor is you've run out of funding.

WOOLLEY. I'm starting a new campaign for donations.

MARKS. A new campaign to build yourself a palace.

WOOLLEY. All respectable institutions have a president's house.

MARKS. I miss you.

WOOLLEY. I miss you too.

5.

(**MARKS** *is smoking outside the library with* **PEARL**.)

MARKS. Yes, but who told you the couplet was necessary?

PEARL. Shakespeare.

MARKS. Inherited forms:

Suspect.

PEARL. What am I supposed to do?

MARKS. Let content demand the form.

Or vice versa.

Experiment.

Get dirty.

PEARL. I want very much to do that.

MARKS. I know you do.

I know you do, Pearl.

PEARL. I feel like I should tell you something.

But I'm embarrassed.

MARKS. Embarrassment:

A social construct to restrict the wingspan of the mind.

PEARL. Yeah.

MARKS. So?

PEARL. You know I'm on work-study.

MARKS. Sure.

PEARL. I'm a linens girl.

MARKS. You're a linens woman.

PEARL. I'm a linens woman.

In Brigham Hall.

MARKS. Oh.

PEARL. Well, there are a couple of us.

MARKS. And?

PEARL. We were turning down the sheets in your room.

MARKS. ...

PEARL. We found your letters.

MARKS. Those are private.

PEARL. I know.

I told the girls not to read them, but.

MARKS. And?

PEARL. I want you to know...

There are a couple of us.

Like you.

And we're all really shipping you and President Woolley. There's like a...fan club.

A secret society.

We've got a mascot and everything.

MARKS. Pearl?

PEARL. Yes, Ms. Marks?

MARKS. I want you to practice living.

PEARL. What?

MARKS. Go out and fuck somebody, Pearl.

PEARL. Why?

MARKS. Because poetry doesn't come out of fan-fiction.

PEARL. I think I'm in love with you.

MARKS. You're not.

PEARL. How are you so sure?

MARKS. You don't know me.

You know the idea of me.

The idea of me is easy to love.

The reality of me is very different.

PEARL. I want to know the reality of you.

MARKS. Get a grip, Pearl.

And stop with the goddamn couplets.

6.

(In the office of the president.)

WOOLLEY. Welsh, I think I'd like to use the Osborne money to get some new textbooks this year. I was just perusing a few in the library – lot of Creationism. I'm thinking we should have some...varying opinions.

WELSH. I'm afraid the Osbornes won't be renewing their contribution this year.

WOOLLEY. They donate every year.

WELSH. Not this year.

WOOLLEY. Did they say why?

WELSH. They did.

WOOLLEY. Out with it, Welsh.

WELSH. They said they fear you're making the school too political.

WOOLLEY. I'm what?

WELSH. They said that they believe you're using the school to push an agenda of your own.

WOOLLEY. And what agenda is that?

WELSH. Well, you've abolished domestic services.

WOOLLEY. I don't think we need to teach our students how to do laundry.

WELSH. You've done away with mandatory chapel.

WOOLLEY. I haven't *done away* with it. I've just reduced it to once a week.
Do you know how insane it is to force our students to go to chapel *every day*?

WELSH. You've fired half the faculty.

WOOLLEY. Retired them.

WELSH. And hired all female professors to replace them.

WOOLLEY. We practice what we preach in my administration.

WELSH. You've replaced equestrian studies
with veterinarian studies.

WOOLLEY. You can't major in horses, Welsh.

WELSH. And the marriage rates of your recent alumnae have so plummeted
that the Osbornes say there is reason to believe
you are somehow instilling in the students
your own views of marriage.

WOOLLEY. My own views of marriage?

WELSH. That's what they said.

WOOLLEY. What do the Osbornes know about my own views of marriage?

WELSH. That's just what they said.

WOOLLEY. Have I ever discussed marriage with the Osbornes in your memory, Welsh?

WELSH. Not in my memory, Madam President.

WOOLLEY. Where are they getting this from?

WELSH. I don't know, Madam President.

WOOLLEY. Surely you have an opinion.
A guess, a theory, a hypothesis,
something.

WELSH. I'm not sure, Madam President,
but it could be because you yourself
are an unmarried woman.

WOOLLEY. Why would my not being married influence the students?

WELSH. Well, they seem to look up to you a great deal.

WOOLLEY. Do they?

WELSH. They do.

WOOLLEY. Well, what can I do about that?
Does the board want me to get married just to influence my students?

WELSH. No one has suggested that, Madam President.

WOOLLEY. Do they want me to tell my students to get married?

WELSH. They might.

WOOLLEY. They want me to tell my students to get married?

That's ridiculous!

I don't tell my students to do anything but their goddamn homework.

WELSH. You did tell them to "reject inherited belief systems" in your last address.

WOOLLEY. I didn't! I told them to *examine*.

Examine them, Welsh.

That's entirely different.

WELSH. My mistake, Madam President.

WOOLLEY. Did the Osbornes mention that?

WELSH. They didn't.

WOOLLEY. But you're mentioning it.

WELSH. I am.

WOOLLEY. Is anyone else mentioning it?

WELSH. They might be.

WOOLLEY. I see...

Other donors?

WELSH. Yes.

WOOLLEY. Why do we have to do this like a riddle every time, Welsh?

Will you just tell me what they're saying?

WELSH. They're saying that you might be trying to upend the concept of womanhood.

WOOLLEY. They miss the old school for wives, eh?

WELSH. They do.

They think perhaps the institution was better as a seminary

than it is as a university.

Women were leaving with less

rebellious ideas.

WOOLLEY. Well, we'll have to do without the Osbornes.

WELSH. It's not just the Osbornes.

WOOLLEY. We'll lose a few donors.

We'll gain a few new ones.

These things balance themselves out.

WELSH. I think you're underestimating this concern.

WOOLLEY. Which concern?

WELSH. That you're making the school too political.

WOOLLEY. What is this complaint?

I don't understand this complaint.

We're a women's college.

We're inherently political.

Can you explain this to me?

WELSH. It's a delicate time in history.

The great war.

WOOLLEY. Wilson says were staying out of the war

WELSH. Still, people are anxious.

It's not a time to be

making waves.

WOOLLEY. Suffrage.

WELSH. They're worried you're going to take a stand.

WOOLLEY. Of course I'm going to take a stand.

WELSH. Madam President, if I may?

WOOLLEY. Yes, go on.

WELSH. It isn't the right moment.

WOOLLEY. There's no such thing as the right moment, Welsh.

That's a fantasy.

WELSH. We're in a very tenuous position.

You've made a lot of changes to the school.

People are anxious.

Alumnae say they don't recognize it.

Donors say they don't agree with it.

Fathers are calling saying they're fighting with their daughters over the holidays.

Women's education is at risk.

People are not happy about this new generation of women coming into the workforce, refusing marriage proposals, leaving their family homes.

WOOLLEY. What am I supposed to do? Coddle their anxieties
about a shifting world?

WELSH. No, of course not.
You're executing your vision.
We can work with that, we can sell that.
But this is not the time or place for you to start
championing outside causes.

WOOLLEY. How many donors are we talking about?

WELSH. I couldn't say.

WOOLLEY. Try.

WELSH. At least half.

WOOLLEY. HALF!

WELSH. Who have made their feelings known.

WOOLLEY. When were you going to bring this up with me?

WELSH. I've made several appointments with you this week
and you've cancelled them all.

WOOLLEY. Well, how about this?
Let's set a little precedent.

If I'm about to lose half of our endowment,
why don't you just walk right in?
Don't make an appointment,
don't call ahead,
you don't even have to knock.

If I'm about to run this place into the ground,
why don't you just *run* in?

(**MARKS** *bursts in, holding a newspaper.*)

MARKS. I'm going to kill myself.

WOOLLEY. Thank you, Dean Welsh.

(**WELSH** *exits.*)

Hi.

(**MARKS** *thrusts the paper at* **WOOLLEY**.)

MARKS. They said my story was self-important gibberish.

WOOLLEY. Sexist fucking pigs.

You think Thoreau wasn't writing self-important gibberish?

MARKS. I think it's this place.

WOOLLEY. Holyoke?

MARKS. I think it's making me stupid.

WOOLLEY. You're not stupid.

MARKS. I think I'm becoming *regional*.

Provincial maybe.

I need to go back to Boston.

WOOLLEY. I'm not sure that that's the answer.

MARKS. If I spend all my time *teaching*,

I'm never going to become a better writer.

WOOLLEY. Yes, but the *reality* of the situation is that you have to support yourself somehow.

MARKS. Maybe I'll get a rich husband.

WOOLLEY. One who doesn't mind that you detest cooking, and laundry, and anything that happens before eleven a.m.

MARKS. Someone who will let me write all day.

And weep.

WOOLLEY. Darling.

MARKS. Don't darling me.

You're killing me.

WOOLLEY. *I'm* killing you?

MARKS. You're making me live here!

In *faculty housing*.

In this stupid fucking place with these stupid fucking people.

And I'm writing self-important gibberish because of it.

WOOLLEY. It was one review.

MARKS. I'm dying.

WOOLLEY. I think you're a gorgeous writer.

MARKS. I don't want to be alive.

WOOLLEY. Your students worship you.

MARKS. I hate my students.

WOOLLEY. You don't.

MARKS. I do.

WOOLLEY. You don't really.

MARKS. I hate everything.

WOOLLEY. Let's go out tonight.

MARKS. I won't be alive tonight.

WOOLLEY. Let's go to an inn for the weekend.

MARKS. Yes, please.

WOOLLEY. Let's drink a lot and be selfish.

MARKS. Yes, please.

WOOLLEY. I'll make you forget everything.

MARKS. Yes, please.

7.

(The morning after an indulgent night.)

*(**MARKS** is in bed.)*

*(**WOOLLEY** is bringing her water.)*

MARKS. oh god my head

WOOLLEY. too much wine

MARKS. my eye, my right eye

WOOLLEY. drink this

MARKS. do you ever become convinced that your organs are turning against you?

WOOLLEY. no, drink this

MARKS. do you ever become so convinced that your body is murdering you that you start to get conspiratorial and sour and you hope to poison your body before it poisons you?

WOOLLEY. and some aspirin

MARKS. do you ever wish your body would just finish the job?

WOOLLEY. you're just hungover

MARKS. I'm dying

WOOLLEY. you're just hungover

MARKS. I wish I was dying

WOOLLEY. you don't

MARKS. I have nothing worth living for

WOOLLEY. gee thanks

MARKS. I don't, I have nothing, what do I have?

WOOLLEY. when you say that do you know what it feels like?

MARKS. what?

WOOLLEY. when you tell me that you have nothing worth living for do you know what I hear?

MARKS. you know what I mean

WOOLLEY. I don't know what you mean. I don't know why I mean so little to you

MARKS. you don't, you don't

WOOLLEY. you have nothing worth living for, you said it yourself

MARKS. you know I love you

WOOLLEY. I don't know that. how would I know that?

MARKS. of course I love you, look at my life, look at everything I've given up for you

WOOLLEY. with resentment

MARKS. well, what am I – a saint? I never wanted to be a wife, you know that

WOOLLEY. I think you can't see beyond yourself

MARKS. oh great. "self-important gibberish."
you and that reviewer should meet up to talk about how terrible I am.

WOOLLEY. I don't think you're terrible
I think you're selfish

MARKS. I'm selfish? you made me move to fucking Holyoke for your career and I'm selfish

WOOLLEY. I carve out space for you, I take care of you, I listen to you

MARKS. oh and I don't take care of you, I don't listen to you

WOOLLEY. no, you don't

MARKS. and what fucking space do you give me? where's the president's house you promised me, my writer's retreat? you promised me a castle and you gave me a dorm

WOOLLEY. I think you need to grow up

MARKS. that's fucking rich. I'm not grown-up enough for you?

WOOLLEY. I want a partner, not a child

MARKS. then maybe you shouldn't date your students, Professor Woolley.

WOOLLEY. that's not fair

MARKS. maybe you should date someone your own age

WOOLLEY. maybe I should

MARKS. do you really want to do this right now?

WOOLLEY. drink some water, take your aspirin, and grow
up

8.

(*A house called Sweet Pea.*)

(**WOOLLEY** *is at the door, with flowers.*)

(**FELICITY** *answers.*)

FELICITY. President Woolley! Please come in.

WOOLLEY. You don't have to call me President Woolley.

FELICITY. Oh!

May I call you Mary?

WOOLLEY. No.

But Woolley is fine.

FELICITY. Okay.

Please come in, Woolley.

WOOLLEY. Thank you.

(**WOOLLEY** *enters.*)

(*It's awkward.*)

(*Neither really knows what to say to the other.*)

It's a sweet house.

FELICITY. Isn't it?

And it's so nice to be free from faculty housing.

WOOLLEY. It's very green.

FELICITY. Yes!

Jeannette and I thought the green was so cute.

That's why we named it Sweet Pea.

WOOLLEY. Sweet Pea.

Cute.

FELICITY. I don't know where she is.

WOOLLEY. It's okay.

She's always late.

FELICITY. That's right – you would know!

WOOLLEY. Yeah.

(Awkward.)

FELICITY. You know, I got a very competitive offer from Wheaton before I came here.

WOOLLEY. Oh yeah?

FELICITY. Yeah, but I had read that piece about you in the...

WOOLLEY. *Atlantic*?

FELICITY. No...

WOOLLEY. *Springfield Review*?

FELICITY. No...

WOOLLEY. The *Times*?

FELICITY. Yes!

And I just thought: this woman is doing something incredible.

As a philosophy professor, I have to say –

*(**MARKS** enters.)*

MARKS. Her head is big enough, Felicity.

*(**MARKS** kisses **WOOLLEY**.)*

Hi.

WOOLLEY. Hi.

FELICITY. I guess I should um.

Make myself scarce.

MARKS. Join us! I'm making dinner.

FELICITY. You don't mind?

*(**WOOLLEY** definitely minds.)*

WOOLLEY. No, not at all.

*(**MARKS** begins to prepare dinner.)*

(It's not pretty.)

MARKS. Felicity, Woolley here is "on the fence" about women's suffrage.

*(**FELICITY** laughs.)*

*(Neither **MARKS** nor **WOOLLEY** laughs.)*

FELICITY. Oh.

Oh my god.

You're serious?

WOOLLEY. I just said I have a few reservations, that's all.

MARKS. She isn't sure it's necessary.

FELICITY. Excuse me, but that's insane.

MARKS. I told you.

WOOLLEY. That's not what I said.

I said I'm not totally sure that that's the position *I* should be taking right now.

FELICITY. The right to vote is the right to have a voice.

Without a voice, we have nothing.

WOOLLEY. I'm just a little more focused on the looming financial crisis.

The great war.

FELICITY. But without the right to vote, you can't do anything about any of those things.

It's essential.

MARKS. She was asked to speak at a suffrage rally.

FELICITY. You have to speak.

WOOLLEY. I'm not sure if I'm the right person.

FELICITY. I guess I'm just kind of stunned.

MARKS. I told you.

FELICITY. Everything you talk about.

The empowerment of women.

The importance of women's education.

Creating fully fleshed out human beings

and not just developing a factory for mindless wives.

MARKS. That's exactly what I said.

What I've been saying.

FELICITY. What about all your talk of revolution?

MARKS. What about it, *Madam* President?

WOOLLEY. I didn't say no to the rally.

I said I'd think about it.

FELICITY. This is it.

This is the big bold direction you're taking us.

This is the next step, this is the actualization of the dream you've been painting for the last ten years. Women with opportunities. Women with autonomy. Women with voices. Women with power.

You could take this moment, and take a position.

And the school could become stronger because of it.

Not weaker.

WOOLLEY. We could lose donors.

FELICITY. And gain new ones.

MARKS. Revolution.

WOOLLEY. I'm still thinking about it.

9.

(The lights shift, it's later.)
*(**FELICITY** is gone.)*
(It's not that night.)
(It's a different night.)
(Or.)
(It's every night of a certain period.)

MARKS. Don't think I haven't noticed

WOOLLEY. Noticed what?

MARKS. You

WOOLLEY. You're not making sense

MARKS. I see you
     and I love you

WOOLLEY. What are you trying to say?

MARKS. I see how you walk
     how you talk
     How you drop "Mary"
     and you evade madam
     and you don't say miss

WOOLLEY. Just say what you mean

MARKS. How you fuck

WOOLLEY. Jeannette, I don't have time for this

MARKS. You've gotten a taste of power,
     you've gotten a voice

     and I'm proud of you
     and I love you

     and if you leave the rest of us behind

     I'll never forgive you

10.

(The county jail.)

(WOOLLEY and WELSH burst in.)

(MARKS, FELICITY, and PEARL are all in jail.)

MARKS. Hi.

FELICITY. Heeeeeeeey.

WOOLLEY. What happened?

WELSH. We heard that several of our students have been arrested for attempting to vote.

MARKS. For exercising a basic right within a democracy.

FELICITY. For protesting.

MARKS. No taxation without representation.

WELSH. We've come to pay the bail.

MARKS. Absolutely not.

FELICITY. Our imprisonment is part of our protest.

WELSH. For our students.

PEARL. Hi.

WELSH. The faculty involved will be swiftly suspended and placed under review.

MARKS. I'm sure that we won't.

WELSH. For endangering our students.

FELICITY. We were teaching them about the right to protest.

MARKS. This was a lesson in civil disobedience.

WELSH. It's not the faculty's place to take on independent studies in disobedience with their students.

MARKS. I disagree, don't you, Madam President?

WOOLLEY. You could have been hurt.

MARKS. We weren't.

WOOLLEY. You put your students at risk.

PEARL. We put ourselves at risk.

MARKS. Sometimes we need to go to extreme measures to be heard.

WOOLLEY. I'm not sure why you didn't speak to me about
this beforehand.

MARKS. I wasn't aware I had to ask your permission.

WOOLLEY. To take my students into a high-risk situation?

PEARL. We took ourselves.

MARKS. I wasn't aware that I needed your permission
to voice my opinion.

WOOLLEY. This is how you voice your opinion?

MARKS. Yes.

WOOLLEY. You're a fucking writer.
You couldn't come up with a better way
to voice your opinion than this?
This is the best thing you could come up with?

FELICITY. Civil disobedience is an effective –

MARKS. This is the first time I've really gotten
under the skin.
This is the first time I seem to be communicating
how important this is to me.

WOOLLEY. How many students are in here?

PEARL. There are six of us.

WOOLLEY. We'll post bail for the six students, Dean Welsh.

WELSH. Agreed, Madam President.

PEARL. Our imprisonment is our –

WOOLLEY. The college is your legal guardian,
you are under my care and
you are leaving immediately.

MARKS. These women still have their rights
they can protest if they'd like.

WOOLLEY. These teenagers have homework to do
so I'm taking them back to their dorms.

My faculty, however, are welcome to
rot in jail
if they so choose.

FELICITY. I thought you'd appreciate what we're doing here.
We're fighting for our rights as women.
This is the revolution in action.

MARKS. Don't bother, Felicity.
She doesn't want a revolution
look at her
she's fine where she is.

WOOLLEY. I don't want a revolution?

MARKS. No, you don't.
You just want power.

WOOLLEY. Oh fuck you, darling.
Maybe you've forgotten
from your seat of privilege
what the rest of the world looks like, but
I am a fucking revolution.

Now get in the carriage, girls.

We'll leave our professors here as long as they'd like.

11.

(Sweet Pea.)

(WOOLLEY *at the door, with flowers.)*

(FELICITY *answers, sees who it is, and walks away.)*

WOOLLEY. I guess I'll just

let myself in.

FELICITY. ...

WOOLLEY. Is Jeannette here?

FELICITY. She's upstairs.

WOOLLEY. Would you mind telling her I'm here?

(FELICITY *calls upstairs loudly and* **MARKS** *answers loudly.)*

(We don't see **MARKS.***)*

FELICITY. JEANNETTE.

MARKS. *(Offstage.)* YEAH?

FELICITY. YOUR BULL IS HERE.

MARKS. *(Offstage.)* I DON'T WANT TO SEE HER.

FELICITY. She's unavailable at the moment.

WOOLLEY. I know she's still mad at me,

but could you just tell her

that I'm sorry.

FELICITY. SHE SAYS SHE'S SORRY.

MARKS. *(Offstage.)* TELL HER TO GO FUCK HERSELF.

FELICITY. I think she's napping.

WOOLLEY. Could you just tell her

she was right.

FELICITY. SHE SAYS YOU WERE RIGHT.

WOOLLEY. Could you just tell her

I'm working on my speech

for the next suffrage rally.

FELICITY. SHE SAYS SHE'S SPEAKING AT THE SUFFRAGE RALLY.

(**MARKS** *starts to come down the stairs.*)

(**WOOLLEY** *doesn't see her.*)

WOOLLEY. Tell her
  I don't have that much written yet
  but I want to start with saying
  something along the lines of
  what a fucking fool I've been
  a coward maybe
  and that although I've been slow
  to take up the cause
  I will be the best champion I can be
  now that –

MARKS. Stop talking.

WOOLLEY. Why?
  Is it terrible?

MARKS. Awful.

  And I'm still really fucking mad at you.

WOOLLEY. I know.
  I fucked up.

MARKS. You really fucked up.

WOOLLEY. I shouldn't have left you there.

MARKS. You should have been in there with us.

WOOLLEY. I'm sorry.
  I lost the forest for the trees.

  Forgive me?

MARKS. Are you really speaking at the rally?

WOOLLEY. I'm the opener.

MARKS. What about your donors? The board?

WOOLLEY. If they don't like it...

  fuck 'em
  we'll figure it out.

12.

WOOLLEY. They loved it

MARKS. Who?

WOOLLEY. The board!
They went nuts for it
everyone
the newspapers.

Now they're saying we have to capitalize on this.

MARKS. On what?

WOOLLEY. This momentum
we came out for suffrage at just the right time
that's what they're saying
it was a political dream scenario –
early enough that we're in the press for it
but late enough that public opinion had already swayed
to our side.

I told them what I've been thinking a lot about lately,

globalism
women's issues worldwide,

they ate it up
they're sending me to China.

MARKS. To China?

WOOLLEY. There's a coalition for Christian women's education
or something.
I don't know but it's the perfect opportunity.
They're evangelizing or whatever
but I'm evangelizing too
equal opportunities for women
this is the next frontier
women worldwide will hear our message.

MARKS. ...

WOOLLEY. Well, don't just stand there
say something.

MARKS. I don't know what to say.

WOOLLEY. You did this!
    Come out for suffrage, you said
    and so I did.

MARKS. Finally.

WOOLLEY. Yes but it was the perfect time
    the amendment is going to pass
    and that momentum is going to carry me
    all the way to China.

MARKS. …

WOOLLEY. Aren't you happy?

MARKS. I feel kind of nauseous, actually.

WOOLLEY. Why?

MARKS. When did you turn into such an opportunist?

WOOLLEY. I'm not an opportunist.

MARKS. What even are your principles anymore?

WOOLLEY. You know what my principles are
    they're the same as yours.

MARKS. I'm not sure that they are.

WOOLLEY. Jeannette, honey,
    what's your vision?

MARKS. Complete equality.

WOOLLEY. And how do you achieve that?

MARKS. It starts with suffrage
    and then we elect women
    and then we end capitalism.

WOOLLEY. But how do you accomplish that?

MARKS. It's the logical answer
    everyone will get there eventually.

WOOLLEY. But how?

MARKS. Impassioned debate.

WOOLLEY. Who do you debate?

MARKS. The other side.

WOOLLEY. Which is everyone.

MARKS. Public debate, two speakers
one issue.

WOOLLEY. How do you get invited?

MARKS. A known expert, an outspoken advocate for
socialism would be invited.

WOOLLEY. How do you become a known expert?

MARKS. Publish works.

WOOLLEY. How do you publish works?

MARKS. Write something remarkable.

WOOLLEY. Who decides it's remarkable?

MARKS. Are you done?

WOOLLEY. I'm just saying,
darling,

it's not a sexy revolution
there's compromise
and hedging.

I'm just being realistic.

MARKS. I feel like I've lost you.
Where's your idealism?

WOOLLEY. Oh I'm still an idealist.
I'm still a horrible romantic.

MARKS. Are you?

WOOLLEY. Nobody but a romantic is stupid enough
to spend their life with another person.

MARKS. Is that what we're doing?

WOOLLEY. Of course it is.

MARKS. It doesn't always feel like that.

WOOLLEY. When the president's house is finished –

MARKS. I hope I live that long.

WOOLLEY. Look
I know this isn't exactly
Camelot
but we are making progress.

Look at how much we've changed since we got here.

MARKS. I don't know if it will ever be enough.

WOOLLEY. Jesus, Jeannette
    this moral superiority,
    hopeless radical thing

    is just sanctimonious defeatism.

    Excuse me for stooping low enough
    to get my hands dirty.

    I'll take a handful of small victories
    over a lifetime of rigid defeat.

    You can have the high ground
    it's all yours.

13.

(**PEARL** *and* **MARKS** *smoking in front of the library.*)

PEARL. Three months is an awfully long time.

MARKS. It's a semester.

PEARL. Has she written?

MARKS. Yes. Of course she's written.

PEARL. Her letters are beautiful.

...From what I've read.

MARKS. I'm glad you don't turn down my linens anymore.

PEARL. I miss it.

The smell of your sheets.

Is that weird?

MARKS. You're a weirdo, Pearl.

PEARL. Could you love me?

MARKS. I thought you were in a secret society of fan-girls for my relationship with President Woolley.

PEARL. I am.

I'm the president.

MARKS. President Pearl.

PEARL. You're into presidents, aren't you Ms. Marks?

MARKS. I need you to settle down.

PEARL. I'll do anything you tell me to.

MARKS. I need you to stop talking to me like this.

PEARL. Anything but that.

MARKS. Here's the thing, Pearl.

I want to expand your horizons.

I really do.

PEARL. Expand them.

MARKS. But I'm just not sure that I should be responsible for *all* of your horizons.

PEARL. Why?

MARKS. Diversify, Pearl.

It's good for you.

14.

(Dean Welsh's office.)

MARKS. I'm starting a new class.

WELSH. You're?

MARKS. I'm starting a playwriting class.

WELSH. That's not really something we do here.

MARKS. Right.
That's why I'm starting it.

WELSH. I'm not sure we have the demand.

MARKS. My classes always have high demand.

WELSH. Yes.
That's true.
Unusually high.
I suspect it has something to do with the cigarettes.
But *playwriting*.
That's not really a field for women.

MARKS. Currently, the only field for women
is a graveyard.

WELSH. That's sort of a morbid view of the world, isn't it,
Ms. Marks?

MARKS. I'm sort of a morbid person.

WELSH. Still, I just don't think we've got the resources for
an entirely new class.
And who would take over Lit 101?

MARKS. Lit 101 could be taught by a caged animal.

WELSH. Ms. Marks.
I think you think you've got a sort of immunity to
propriety.
Because of your cozy position with President Woolley.

MARKS. I think I have an immunity to propriety
because I'm good at what I do.
Because my students leave my classes with a greater
sense
of themselves and the world.

And I think I have a pretty great fucking track record of helping students find their voices.

My student poetry series sells like a fucking jazz concert. Please don't infantilize me.

Please don't accredit my success to President Woolley.

I have a vision of my own.

I am going to help women find greater access to themselves.

I'm going to show them that the full scope of humanity is available to them.

That they can be heroes and villains and lovers and fools.

And it starts with a playwriting class.

WELSH. I have to deny your request at this time.

MARKS. Why?

WELSH. It's an issue of space.

When President Woolley returns from China you can raise the question with her. Of course, now that she's extended her trip...

MARKS. Extended?

WELSH. Oh. You didn't hear?

We just got a telegram.

Another three months, *at least*.

MARKS. I see.

Thank you so much for your time, Dean Welsh.

WELSH. My pleasure, Ms. Marks.

15.

(**WOOLLEY** *in China.*)

WOOLLEY. I'm standing on a small steamboat in a wide
river.
White rocks on either side, sloping
you can see the past written in lines of salt and tide.
you can see that in the winter the river floods
twenty feet higher than the water as it lays now
coolly wrapping down the side of this island

I am being given a brief history of the island
by an elegant guide: a Chinese alum
the rest of the committee is very impressed
that everywhere we go I find one of our own
and she is – without fail – well poised and generous

And I am showing the sort of interest I am famous for
showing
the intent gaze and the nodding and the asking of
interesting questions
that the speaker is thrilled to answer

but in reality I am gazing down the wide river and I am
thinking only
of you, half a world away, and forever mine
and I am puzzling over that inexplicable cord that holds
us together

when just at that moment I am interrupted
by a strange barking
and there I see, halfway down the river,
a large elegant swan swimming downstream

and the alum is thrilled, she takes the opportunity to
tell us
all about the history of the bird
and then suddenly

there is another swan coming down the river
and

I remember in that instant
the miracle of the swan and other animals
is that they somehow manage
even out on a wild and wide Chinese river
even among predators and prey
even at the mercy of the elements
they somehow manage to mate for life

and just then the second swan barks and honks and
flaps her wings
and takes off in the opposite direction
and the first swan, who had been so deliberately
moving downstream,
now honks a little and looks longingly down the river,
but ultimately turns around and swims back up
against the current

and then, of course, I am struck again
by the second miracle of swans which is
how gracious and elegant they look above the surface
of the water
while down below they must be
churning relentlessly
to go against such a strong current
while maintaining their poise

it is a thought I can't hold onto for as long as I'd like
because soon I am drawn back
to the art of asking questions
and the answers come in quick succession
while I look longingly down the river
and try to pretend I cannot hear you
calling me home
from half a world away

16.

(**MARKS** *in bed with* **PEARL** *in her room at Sweet Pea.*)

PEARL. Can I read some of her letters?

MARKS. That feels like a violation.

PEARL. Really?

MARKS. Yes.

PEARL. Okay.

MARKS. Besides, why would you want to read her letters to me?

PEARL. For the society.

We've been low on material.

Since the China trip.

It feels so long.

It feels like such a long time.

And when we heard the trip had been extended we were just...

beside ourselves.

We're hurting.

MARKS. You're hurting, huh?

PEARL. I mean.

I don't mean to compare our pain to yours.

MARKS. Can we talk about a few things?

PEARL. Anything.

MARKS. Can you try to refrain from speaking in the plural first person?

Like as if you're speaking on behalf of a collective?

It makes me feel like I'm sleeping with a hive.

PEARL. Okay.

MARKS. You're not reporting on this?

To your society.

Are you?

PEARL. Oh god no.

I would be excommunicated.

MARKS. You would?

PEARL. I would.

MARKS. Why?

PEARL. We swore a solemn oath to support and uphold your relationship.

MARKS. Why would you do that?

PEARL. We ship you.
　Plain and simple.

MARKS. You're such a weirdo, Pearl.

PEARL. Which is why, of course,
　I'm feeling conflicted.
　About my solemn oath
　and how it lies in direct opposition
　to my new position as your lover,
　who poses a serious threat
　to your relationship,
　which I adore and respect
　and ship.

MARKS. Yes.
　Let's talk about that.

PEARL. Talk about –?

MARKS. This.

　Is sort of.

　An educational experience.

　An independent study.

　In independence.

　Among other things.

PEARL. I see.

MARKS. It's an extension of...

　your education.

PEARL. Right.

MARKS. This isn't...
　a relationship.

PEARL. Oh.

MARKS. This is...

A mentorship.

And you don't pose a serious risk to my relationship.

In fact,

you could view this,

if you wanted,

as a practical application

to your theoretical oath.

This is a way in which you are...

supporting my relationship.

Do you understand?

PEARL. I think I do.

MARKS. Good.

That's good, Pearl.

17.

(Sweet Pea.)
(**WOOLLEY** *is at the door, with flowers.)*
(**FELICITY** *answers.)*

FELICITY. Oh!!
You're back!

WOOLLEY. I'm back!

FELICITY. Oh my god!
That's so great!
How was China?

WOOLLEY. It was interesting.
A long trip.
The world is round.
The world is so big.
And yet I've never felt that it was smaller – does that make sense?

FELICITY. It does.
Philosophy, remember?

WOOLLEY. Of course.

(An awkward moment of silence.)

Is Jeannette here?

FELICITY. Yes.
Of course.
Let me...

Is she expecting you?

WOOLLEY. No, nobody is.
I was supposed to get in next week,
but I couldn't take it anymore.
I took an earlier freighter.

FELICITY. Right.

Let me just...
Do you want something to drink?

WOOLLEY. No. Thank you.

FELICITY. Okay.

Take a seat.

I'll just...

> (**FELICITY** *runs upstairs.*)
>
> (**WOOLLEY** *sits, holding flowers.*)
>
> (*An awkward amount of time passes.*)
>
> (**FELICITY** *tries to come downstairs coolly.*)

She'll be right down.

WOOLLEY. She always takes her time, doesn't she?

> (**FELICITY** *laughs.*)
>
> (*Too much.*)

FELICITY. Jeannette, Jeannette.

So tell me more! About...China.

WOOLLEY. What about it?

FELICITY. The...philosophy.

> (**MARKS** *comes downstairs.*)

MARKS. Who is this handsome stranger in my house holding flowers?

WOOLLEY. Hi there.

MARKS. Hi.

FELICITY. So I'll get going.

WOOLLEY.	**MARKS.**
Yes.	No.

FELICITY. Okay.

MARKS. You can stay for a second.

Or no! We'll go.

Let's go for a walk, *President Woolley.*

WOOLLEY. Okay.

FELICITY. Okay.

And I will.

Stay here.

WOOLLEY. Is everything okay?

You both seem like you've seen a ghost.

FELICITY. No ghosts! Just presidents.

MARKS. One president.

You.

Just you.

You handsome devil.

Let's go.

(A sound from upstairs.)

WOOLLEY. Is something wrong?

FELICITY. Nope.

WOOLLEY. Is someone upstairs?

FELICITY. That's absurd. No one is upstairs.

WOOLLEY. I see.

Well, isn't that wonderful.

Isn't that beautiful.

FELICITY. I got a cat.

WOOLLEY. Right.

What's her name?

MARKS. Pearl.

FELICITY. Is the name of my cat.

WOOLLEY. How long?

FELICITY. She is three months old.

MARKS. Felicity.

You can drop the cat thing.

FELICITY. Okay. I'm going to go.

*(**FELICITY** exits.)*

MARKS. Since I heard about the extension of your trip from
Dean Welsh.

WOOLLEY. I wrote to you as soon as it was decided.

MARKS. But you telegrammed Dean Welsh.

WOOLLEY. No, the board telegrammed Dean Welsh.

MARKS. And you didn't write to me before you decided.

You didn't ask for my opinion.

You didn't ask if I was dying here without you.

WOOLLEY. So this is my fault?

MARKS. This isn't anyone's fault.

This isn't anything.

This is just Pearl.

WOOLLEY. Bad couplets Pearl?

You're sleeping with your student now?

That's – you could be fired for that.

MARKS. Oh really, Professor Woolley?

Is that so unfamiliar to you?

WOOLLEY. Okay.

I think we need some air.

I think I just need a second.

I think this is just happening.

Fast.

Quickly.

I think I just need –

18.

(Moment in love.)
(In the beginning.)
(At the end.)
(Who are you.)
(**WOOLLEY** *is holding some literature.)*
(**MARKS** *is young, so young.)*

WOOLLEY. I've been doing some reading

MARKS. you didn't get *this* from Wellesley's library

where did you find it?

WOOLLEY. does it matter?

MARKS. it does, you're a professor, you want to be a dean, if people knew –

WOOLLEY. people know

MARKS. yes but they don't know *what* it is, they don't even know what to imagine we do

WOOLLEY. they still don't, I got this from a friend

MARKS. a friend?

WOOLLEY. yes, an old friend

MARKS. "an old friend"

WOOLLEY. Jeannette...

MARKS. I wasn't aware you had old friends

WOOLLEY. of course I have old friends

MARKS. like me? old friends like me?

WOOLLEY. no, no one is like you

MARKS. close friends, literature-sharing friends?

WOOLLEY. yes

MARKS. why is this only coming up now?

WOOLLEY. I didn't think it was important
– to our relationship

MARKS. you don't get to just decide that

WOOLLEY. you never asked

MARKS. I assumed you would have told me

WOOLLEY. why would I have told you?

MARKS. because! I don't know, I thought –

WOOLLEY. it's the past

MARKS. you're my only past

WOOLLEY. I know

MARKS. I hate you for that

WOOLLEY. you hate me?

MARKS. because you know how to live without me, but I have no idea how to live without you

WOOLLEY. you don't have to, you'll never have to

MARKS. you don't know that

WOOLLEY. yes, I do, I love you, I'll never leave you

MARKS. what happened to your old friends?

WOOLLEY. what do you mean?

MARKS. did you promise them forever?

WOOLLEY. that was different. I was younger

MARKS. like me

WOOLLEY. yes, like you

MARKS. so how do you know I won't break your heart?

WOOLLEY. I don't

MARKS. how did you break their hearts?

WOOLLEY. gently

MARKS. really?

WOOLLEY. no, not always. Some people demand a sort of violence

MARKS. violence?

WOOLLEY. emotional violence, rupture

MARKS. tell me what you said to them

WOOLLEY. that's private, buried

MARKS. nothing of yours should be private from me

WOOLLEY. but some of it is

MARKS. I hate you for existing before I met you

WOOLLEY. I'm sorry

MARKS. was it terrible?

WOOLLEY. awful

MARKS. good, that's good

I hope it was miserable

WOOLLEY. it was

it was absolutely devastating

MARKS. tell me one thing you said when you broke someone's heart

WOOLLEY. why?

MARKS. so I know what it sounds like

WOOLLEY. I won't break your heart

MARKS. I just need to know what the words sound like

WOOLLEY. why?

MARKS. so I can prepare

study

WOOLLEY. I'm telling you

MARKS. you have an advantage, you have history

I only have you

tell me

WOOLLEY. Well, there was Lydia...

MARKS. Lydia. What a terrible name.

WOOLLEY. She loved me but I didn't love her

MARKS. How did you know that?

WOOLLEY. Know what?

MARKS. How did you know that she loved you but you didn't love her?

WOOLLEY. She was always trying to see me and I was always trying to avoid her

MARKS. Then why were you dating?

WOOLLEY. It was different, of course, in the beginning.

MARKS. What do you mean of course

WOOLLEY. There was an initial attraction

that was...very strong

MARKS. Then what happened?

WOOLLEY. I got to know her

MARKS. ...that's the most awful thing I've ever heard you say

WOOLLEY. love is ugly

MARKS. what did you say to her?

WOOLLEY. I said: Lydia. I'm not happy. Are you happy? Honestly?

MARKS. what did she say?

WOOLLEY. I don't remember

MARKS. You just forgot? that's pretty heartless

WOOLLEY. She said a lot of things, I was trying to stick to my guns,
I was nervous, she was very...volatile

MARKS. Were there more?

WOOLLEY. ...yes.

MARKS. How many?

WOOLLEY. A few

MARKS. Tell me one more

WOOLLEY. I think one is enough.

MARKS. One more

WOOLLEY. there was Sylvia.

MARKS. "Sylvia" the way you say her name

WOOLLEY. She was my first

MARKS. And?

WOOLLEY. She was a coward

MARKS. What does that mean?

WOOLLEY. She stopped loving me but waited for me to notice

MARKS. How did you notice?

WOOLLEY. First it felt like I was dying
but then I wouldn't die

MARKS. then what happened

WOOLLEY. she made me say the words

MARKS. which words

WOOLLEY. it's like you don't even see me anymore
I'm in the room with you
but you don't see me

MARKS. that sounds terrible

WOOLLEY. it was

MARKS. how did you recover?

WOOLLEY. slowly

and

Lydia

19.

*(**PEARL** is throwing rocks at Marks' window.)*
*(**MARKS** opens the window.)*
*(**PEARL** has to shout for **MARKS** to hear her.)*
*(We all hope **PEARL** is drunk.)*

PEARL. Please
    love me or leave me
    this in-between is unbearable
    I can't bare it
    or you
    or myself
    when I feel like this

    I have never felt so murderous and strange
    before this moment

    I want to kill you
    I love you so much

    stop touching me
    don't ever touch me again
    never stop touching me
    die with me
    stop breathing
    don't you dare breathe another breath
    without me

    if you decide not to love me
    I am going to enter the library
    and open fire

    there is no point in any of this

    I want my love to mar an institution

    I love you so much
    I wish the earth would shrivel up and die

I hate you so fucking much
I want to kill you
by making love to you.
I want to drown you in my tears
violently

I want to hold you down
until you stop breathing

I want your final word
to come out of your mouth
in a bubble from under the water
I want it to be my name
and "please"

I want you to beg me
I want to deny you

I want you to be publicly flogged
and then I'll kiss every wound
and every wound will have my name
and you'll never leave me
or love anyone else

and then I'll die
I'll die so quickly and violently
you'll miss me
you'll miss me forever
your whole life will collapse
and you'll have a hole
a Pearl-shaped hole
in your heart
in your life
you'll circle it at night crying
you'll sing funeral songs
in your sleep

your life will become a dirge

a funeral march

I'll burn myself on a stake
on a pike
like a witch

even though you and I both know
you're the witch
you've cast a spell on me
it makes me crazy
the only antidote
the only way to break through

is to murder us both
is this too much?
have I shown you the unbearable contents of my heart
my real heart
and now you feel that you can neither
look away
nor look directly at me?

I wish you never ever looked at me.
I wish you never touched me.
I wish you never said my name so sweetly.
I wish you never existed

because now everything is so fucking unbearable

I feel so drawn to death to dying

I want the world to suffer
and fall apart

I'm praying for another flood
one of those god-given floods
that wipes out the entire earth

let's drown together

please, no
why are you closing your window,

you heartless witch

don't you see how much I love you?

20.

(**MARKS** *is teaching a class.*)

MARKS. Orlando has just become a woman
and she's trying to figure out
what it means
to be a woman
and suddenly
she thinks of Sasha,
the woman in Russian trousers

why

Sasha broke her heart
hundreds of years ago

and

Orlando has done so much since then

she's sworn off love and other people for a hundred
years *at least*
she's sat under trees and pondered for another hundred
she's decided to be a poet
then been so rejected
she's given it up completely
she's filled her house with everything she could
everything that would fit
she's traveled
she's been an ambassador in Constantinople
she's hosted parties
she's been revolted against
she's died twice for a week each time
she's changed her sex
she's married a gypsy
she's traveled in their caravan
she's been outcast again and again

and yet she's on a boat back to England
and she's thinking of what it means to be a woman
and she thinks of love and what it means to love
and so of course
she thinks
of Sasha
she thinks she loves her more now that she's a woman
she thinks she understands her more
not less

and she passes the river where she met her
during the great freeze
and then the river where Sasha broke her heart
where she betrayed her

hundreds of years later
and Orlando still doesn't know

why

Sasha why would you do that

why would you tear out the heart of Orlando
who every other character in the book
would love
who anyone would be a fool not to love

but Orlando
she can't love any of them
she can love no one

but Sasha

Sasha who left her

who left her there
with her heart torn out
on the night the great freeze
unfroze

    (**MARKS** *is so consumed by this.*)

(She doesn't remember where she is.)
(And then.)
(Finally.)
(She remembers.)

MARKS. class dismissed

21.

(They have finally finished building the president's house.)

*(**MARKS** and **WOOLLEY** explore it.)*

MARKS. It's a palace.

WOOLLEY. A house for a president.

MARKS. President Woolley.

WOOLLEY. And Jeannette Marks.

MARKS. They're not putting *my* name on the door.

WOOLLEY. It's your house too.

MARKS. I'd like a space.
   Of my own still.

WOOLLEY. Besides the house?

MARKS. No.
   Inside the house.

WOOLLEY. You can have any room.

MARKS. The attic.
   Is nice.
   For writing.
   I'll write there I think.

WOOLLEY. A writer's retreat.
   In the president's house.
   As promised.

MARKS. Just thirty years late.

WOOLLEY. I did my best.

   Funding is fickle.

MARKS. It's okay.

   I think it'll be the perfect space
   for the playwriting class I want to start.

WOOLLEY. Oh yeah?

MARKS. Yeah. I was thinking...
   My students are so dramatic.

At this age.

I think they'd spend all day
writing and weeping
if they could.

WOOLLEY. I remember how young writers are.

I remember a certain young writer.

Writing and weeping.

MARKS. I think the attic could maybe be a good alternative
to the classroom.

WOOLLEY. You want them here?

In our house?

MARKS. Yes.

I want to get rid of the invisible line between student
and teacher.

I'm interested in erosion.

WOOLLEY. Okay.

If that's what you want.

22.

(Marks' playwriting class.)

MARKS. I want you to think of a time.
I want you to think of a time
when you were happy.
Completely happy.
Or mostly happy.
Or you thought you were miserable.
But now, with retrospect and
a deeper more evolved understanding
of misery
you realize that you were actually happy.
You realize now that that was what happiness was.

Think back to that moment
of happiness.

What did the room look like?
What did it sound like?
What did it smell like?

Put yourself in the room.
Imagine it.
Feel it.

And now,
imagine,
in another room

a voice starts calling to you.

WOOLLEY. *(Calling from another room.)* Jeannette?

MARKS. What are they saying?

WOOLLEY. Jeannette, honey?
You won't believe this.
I just got a call from Herbert Hoover.

MARKS. Who is it?
What does this person mean to you?

WOOLLEY. They want me to go to peace talks with Hitler.

MARKS. What are they saying?

What does it mean to you?

WOOLLEY. I'm the only woman they've tapped.

They think I might have a different perspective – that's how they put it.

MARKS. Why is this significant?

WOOLLEY. They said I was the leader of the preeminent school of critical social thought.

For women.

That's what they called me.

MARKS. What does this mean?

To you.

What does this mean to you?

Write.

> (**MARKS** *writes.*)
>
> (*She writes and writes.*)
>
> (*Time passes.*)
>
> (**WOOLLEY** *enters.*)

How did it go?

WOOLLEY. They want a woman's touch, they tell me

– what does that mean?

surely they haven't met me,

they'd disqualify me in an instant,

me with my swashbuckling

me with my wide stance

and my take-no-prisoners

bull-in-a-china-shop

attitude –

they want a woman's touch

do they imagine I'll put on a matronly voice

and say Adoooolf

like his mother sending him to his room?

in my fantasy I swagger up to him
grab him by his collar

and put his face against the radiator
until he begs
me begs me

to let him go

and I say,
get the fuck out of Poland,
you motherfucking monster

and I go to put my cigar out on him
and then, finally, he acquiesces

he says,
fine, fine,
we're going
we're getting out
we're not superior to anyone
we get it, we get it
we're sad don't you see
don't you see how fucking sad we are

and I say
being miserable isn't an excuse to be a monster
suffering doesn't allow suffering
you heartless piece of shit

you big pile of shit

(in my mind, as I say this, a violin is swelling, a drum
throbs like a heartbeat)

instead he doesn't even show up
we have our peace talks with Hitler
without Hitler
he sends an envoy
even the envoy walks out early

and I'm not allowed in the smoking room
even though I bet I packed more cigars than
the fucking French at least

and I'm seated with the wives at dinner
they ask me if I have a favorite recipe

I say yes, I've really been perfecting the recipe
for enlightenment
it's a dash of no fucks given
and a pinch of original thought

except
I don't say that
I don't say anything like that

I tell them I put rolled oats in my cookies
they smile a knowing smile

even now I'm wondering
what did that smile mean?

and how is it possible for one person
to be so at odds with every room
they're in?

MARKS. Did you deliver the letters at least?

WOOLLEY. One million letters from women all over the
world
calling for peace
calling for all nations to disarm.

I did.

MARKS. And?

WOOLLEY. Every nation agreed to it on one account.

MARKS. Which was?

WOOLLEY. Not theirs.

MARKS. Didn't it seem like there was a moment
like maybe we were heading toward
I don't know

enlightenment?

WOOLLEY. Maybe not enlightenment

but progress, at least
we've made progress, haven't we?

We're in the president's house
just like I said.

MARKS. We are.

WOOLLEY. That's something.

23.

(The president's office.)
(PRESIDENT WOOLLEY *and* **DEAN WELSH.)**

WOOLLEY. A family man.
You've got to be kidding me.

WELSH. I'm not, no.
That's what they're looking for.

WOOLLEY. What can a family man possibly know about leading a women's college?

WELSH. It's about the image they're trying to promote.

WOOLLEY. What image?
A world with a man in charge?
A school for wives?

WELSH. Family values.

WOOLLEY. And I'm not giving them family values.

WELSH. Your relationship with Ms. Marks has come under some scrutiny of late.

WOOLLEY. Has it?

WELSH. It has.

WOOLLEY. I don't see why now that would suddenly be a problem.
We've been the same all this time.

WELSH. I'm afraid my hands are tied.
This is coming directly from the trustees.

WOOLLEY. But even if they want to replace me,
they can't in good conscience replace me with a man.
This is a university built on the tenets of women's empowerment.
I am, I have always been, scorching a path
for women to follow.

WELSH. Scorching, yes.
That's an apt word.

WOOLLEY. There are qualified women, Welsh.

I know. I've been educating them for thirty-five years.

WELSH. I know that, Madam President.

I raised the same point.

But

it's a delicate time in history

post-war, pre-war

there's been so much turmoil...

The trustees think we should try to restore some order.

The trustees think we need to remember some essential things.

Like the importance of family.

Like the importance of *gracious womanhood*.

WOOLLEY. What does that even mean?

WELSH. They'd like this to end amicably.

WOOLLEY. Of course they would.

WELSH. The severance will be generous.

WOOLLEY. It better be.

WELSH. I'm sorry, Madam President.

I didn't want it to end like this.

24.

(**MARKS** *and* **WOOLLEY** – *on the telephone in two different places.*)

MARKS. There were marches on the streets, honey.

WOOLLEY. Yeah?

MARKS. Walkouts all over campus.

WOOLLEY. Your doing, I'm guessing.

MARKS. Not all of it.

WOOLLEY. Don't stir up too much trouble.
You know Dean Welsh has been dying to get rid of you since you started.
And I'm sure the new president is not going to love you.

MARKS. I'll give him hell. What do I care? I'm tenured.

I still wonder if I should have left with you.
I should have maybe. On principle.

WOOLLEY. You like teaching.

MARKS. It's just that I love my students.

WOOLLEY. How were the plays?

MARKS. Oh you should have seen them.

WOOLLEY. I wish I could have.

MARKS. Who would have thought I would have outlasted you?

WOOLLEY. Not me.

MARKS. My poor bull.
Finally expelled from the china shop.

WOOLLEY. Too much revolution I guess.

MARKS. Or not enough.
I can't tell which way to think of it.

WOOLLEY. You'll visit soon?

MARKS. I will.
And I'll retire soon.

WOOLLEY. No, stay.
You love teaching.
I'm fine.

MARKS. President Woolley?
WOOLLEY. Yes, Ms. Marks?
MARKS. I really do love you.
    They're fools to lose you.
WOOLLEY. I know, darling.
    The boot just fell.
    Something good has got to be coming.
    Later, much later.
    I love you too.